WORKING FOR THE BIG, BAD WOLF

Olive Spencer

Copyright © 2023 Olive Spencer

All rights reserved. This book or any portion thereof may not be reproduced or used in any manner whatsoever without the express written permission of the publisher except for the use of brief quotations in a book review.

First printing, 2023.
Second Edition, 2024

Ruthless Publishing
807 Holmes Drive, Studio LR
Colorado Springs, CO, 80909

www.olivespencer.com
www.olivespencer.medium.com

Also by Olive Spencer

Contemporary Erotica
More than Words
A Dolly for Christmas

Paranormal Erotica
Blood Lust
Blood Lust Crimson Temptations
Ghosted

Erotic Romance
Working for the Big Bad Wolf
Taming the Big Bad Wolf
Old Enough to Know Better

Freebies:
Plaything – Working for the Big Bad Wolf
Playing Telephone – Working for the Big Bad Wolf
Blow Me, Harkness – Ghosted
Feeding Frenzy – Blood Lust

Dedication

For the girls who always wanted the man they couldn't have, this one is for you.

Content Warning

This book contains sex between two consenting adults. While Mina may call Grant her 'uncle' there is no blood relation between them.

Contents

Prologue	1
Chapter One	2
Chapter Two	6
Chapter Three	12
Chapter Four	19
Chapter Five	23
Chapter Six	28
Chapter Seven	34
Chapter Eight	39
Chapter Nine	44
Epilogue	48
Acknowledgements	55
About the Author	57
Where to Find Olive Online	59

Prologue

She was everything I wasn't supposed to want. Young, pretty, a virgin, and my best friend's daughter.

When she walked into my office to ask me for a summer internship, I had only one thing on my mind. Watching her stroll into my workplace in an impossibly tiny skirt and too-tight, white shirt awakened the beast inside of me. I've fought long and hard to keep myself in check, but something about my best friend's little girl has me hot and bothered. Every inch of her draws me in like a Venus Flytrap, waiting to snap. She knows what she's doing, and, by God, she does it well.

I don't want to be her boss. It's an HR disaster waiting to happen.

I don't want to be her honorary uncle. Uncles don't do to their nieces what I want to do to her.

I don't want to sit by and watch her tease me every day. I want to punish her for her bratty ways.

I want my best friend's little girl, and I always get what I want.

They call me the big, bad wolf for a reason.

Chapter One

It's an ordinary Tuesday. My secretary, Gladys, goes over my daily schedule, detailing the day's meetings, when one name jumps out at me. Mina Maguire, my best friend's daughter. Her name lands on me like a blow to the head, and my heart begins to race. I haven't seen Mina since she graduated high school, what was it? Four years ago? She lived up to the stereotype about blondes having more fun, causing her dad more trouble in her teen years than I thought one child could cause. What is she doing, coming to see me?

Gladys continues to go over the day's events, but my mind begins to wander. What could my best friend's daughter possibly want with me? Why would she come here? I don't have time to ponder it in depth before my first meeting starts. The rest of the board of my company, Wolf Industries, strolls into the conference room. They take their seats and stare at me expectantly, waiting for me to start. I shake all thoughts of Mina from my mind and let my business brain take over.

Commanding the boardroom comes as second nature to

me. My alpha mentality makes it easy to control my pack of cynical, snarky, snarling board members when they become unruly. Commanding my thoughts is something entirely different. Several times during the presentation, I find my mind straying as thoughts of her flow into my stream of consciousness. Mina has to be in her early twenties by now, and in college, if I remember right. Does she need a job? Is her dad sick? I have so many questions and so few answers.

At 11:30, there's a short break between meetings, and I stop to catch my breath. I've been at it today since I woke up: answering texts, firing off emails, commanding my troops, and running an empire. The coffee Gladys brought has long gone cold and bitter, but I drink it anyway, hoping for a boost of energy before my next engagement. I have to stay sharp; Wolf Industries doesn't run itself. I fire off more texts and emails in between sips until my cup is as empty as my inbox.

At noon, on the dot, Gladys rings my office line.

I answer the phone cordially. "Yes, Gladys?"

"Mr. Wolf, your twelve o'clock is here. Should I send them in?"

"Go right ahead. My door is open." I keep my office door shut at all times, but Gladys catches my meaning.

The large, frosted-glass doors push open, and a stunning young woman steps into my office. I don't recognize her. She must be a new hire. So new, in fact, that she doesn't have a badge. Her shirt is practically see-through, and her skirt is impossibly tight. She's incredibly inappropriate for this setting, and I'm wondering who sent her.

"And who might you be?" I eye her curiously, wondering

what she's doing here. I thumb through the papers on my desk, trying to figure out who my twelve is and why this gorgeous young woman is suddenly in my office.

"Uncle Grant, don't you remember me?"

Uncle Grant? Oh, God.

"Little Mina? Is that really you? My God, how you've grown." I rise from behind my desk and cross the floor to greet her. Mina grins and wraps her arms around me, pulling me in for a tight, almost-lingering hug. She pulls back, and I finally get a good look at her.

No longer the gangly girl with baby weight in her cherubic cheeks, Mina has blossomed into a grown woman. I look her up and down, appraising her. Her hair is long and carefully styled, framing her delicate features. She wears horn-rimmed glasses, making her look every inch the serious businesswoman and sexy librarian all at once. Her freckles have faded, but, if I look closely enough, I can still see a trail of them dotting across her dainty nose. She's captivating in her beauty, and my heart jumps into my throat.

"Please, just Mina. Only my dad still calls me Little Mina," she says with a soft giggle. I watch a cherry-blossom-pink blush spread across her face, and I find myself staring for a moment too long. Mina's eyes flick to mine, and she tucks a strand of hair behind her ear before straightening up and becoming all business.

"Mina, you've grown up. This is the last thing I expected when Gladys told me you were on today's docket." Her shirt is so sheer, I can make out the neckline of her slip beneath it. And her skirt? When she moves, I can see it ripple around the generous curve of her ass. "Come, have a seat."

I guide her toward the large leather chairs in the center of my office and slyly adjust myself before joining her. The sight of her all grown up has me uncomfortably warm beneath the collar, and I find my slacks fit a little tighter. I need to clear my mind before I get myself into trouble.

Mina takes a seat and crosses her legs, and I catch sight of the seam in her stockings. I stifle a groan and try to get my head back in the game. Mina is here for a reason, and I intend to find out what it is.

"Let me guess, you were expecting baby fat and pigtails?" She giggles, and the sound runs through me. It takes a considerable amount of strength not to stare at the beautiful, shapely woman before me.

I clear my throat and crack a grin. "Well, yes, actually. I was expecting the young woman I last saw at her high school graduation. I was expecting…"

"A little girl? Well, Uncle Grant, I hate to break it to you, but I'm a grown woman now. A grown woman, with grown-woman needs."

I choke and sputter, and Mina looks at me with mischief in her emerald eyes.

"I need a job, Uncle Grant."

Chapter Two

"A job?" I quirk my eyebrow and smirk. I should have known she wasn't coming to me for anything more than something strictly above board. I almost breathe a sigh of relief and stop short.

"A job," she says resolutely. "Specifically, an internship this summer. My degree depends on it."

"An education is important, above all things. You should always be educated," I concede thoughtfully. I study Mina with a careful eye, saying nothing for a long moment while I consider it. Of course, Wolf Industries offers a competitive internship program. It's one of the most sought-after programs in the country, so I shouldn't be surprised she's come to me for it.

"So, that's why you came to visit your dad's best friend? Here I was, thinking you just wanted to catch up. I'm so glad you didn't have any ulterior motives." I let out a laugh and Mina smiles, her face lighting up as she visibly relaxes. The steel in her spine uncoils, and she laughs along with me.

"Oh, I have my motives…" Mina shifts in her chair and leans forward. I catch sight of a slice of ivory skin beneath her blouse and drag my eyes up her face carefully, hoping she can't read my mind. I want to see what's beneath her slip. I want to find out here and now if the rest of her body is just as creamy as the tops of her breasts.

"Uncle Grant," she begins, and I cut her off with a wave of my hand.

"Please, you don't have to call me uncle anymore. We're both adults here, Mina. Grant is just fine."

Mina blushes carnation pink. The color spreads from her cheeks to the tip of her ears as she brushes an errant strand of hair out of her face. She glances up at me with those deep, juniper eyes and licks her lips, tracing the outline with the tip of her tongue. It's so pink, I thought it was a piece of bubblegum.

"Grant, I really need this internship. I'll do anything to work for Wolf. I'll start in the mailroom if need be. It would look stellar on my resume and give me great leveraging power when I apply for jobs in December. I'm graduating a semester early and—"

"Early graduation? You have your mother's looks and your father's brains," I marvel, and Mina flushes again. I take satisfaction in the way the color spreads over her cheeks. For a moment, the flash of an image passes before my eyes, and I have to look away. I imagine Mina laid across my glass-top desk, skirt pulled down, her bare bottom in the air. My hand striking her cheeks, turning her skin rosy with each swipe, her cries filling the air. It's a delicious image, one I'm dying to act out, but I remind myself of my place. This is not the time for such thoughts, no matter how hot they may be.

I clear my throat and lean in, spreading my legs and steepling my fingers beneath my chin as I think. I can't put Mina in the mailroom. It's a waste of my time and her talents, but it'll keep her far, far away from me. My better angels know I should keep her an arm's length away, but I don't listen to them. The devil on my shoulder takes over. I want Mina within eyesight and earshot at all times. An idea strikes me, and I let out an audible 'aha!'

"Mina, how are your secretarial skills? My right hand, Gladys, will be taking a leave of absence in the coming weeks, and I'll need someone to take her place."

"Secretarial?" Mina eyes me with confusion. I can almost see her heart sink through her incredibly thin top, and I rush to clarify.

"Oh, it wouldn't be too demanding. Keep track of my schedule, answer the phones, take dick…" I cough and sputter and quickly correct myself. "Dictation. You'd be taking dictation of memos, inter-office communications, notes to the board, my dry-cleaning list…"

"So I'd be your errand girl?"

I laugh, and Mina relaxes. "No, you'd become my second in command in this office. While I have the board to run Wolf Industries' daily affairs, this office is solely my domain. Every meeting, every phone call, every guest that walks through those doors gets Gladys' approval, and, in her absence, they would require yours. You would hold the keys to the kingdom, as it were."

Mina swallows and nods her head. "Being a secretary isn't exactly in my wheelhouse…"

"No, and I recognize your talents would be better used elsewhere. But the experience of working directly for the CEO of a Fortune 500 company will be invaluable on your resume. It will make other companies jump and take notice when you walk through their doors," I reassure her.

"Would I always be behind the desk, or would there be opportunities to work outside of the office?"

I shake my head. "No no, it won't always be secretarial. You'll accompany me to meetings, client lunches, do on-site visits while they're building our new headquarters across town…" I smile fondly, remembering her childhood. "You had the best dollhouses as a girl, with such an impeccable eye for interior design. It'll require your input, of course."

Mina looks at me with those big green eyes, and I feel myself stiffen. I imagine her looking up at me from below my desk, my dick down her throat. Hastily, I remind myself that I can look, I can imagine, but under no circumstances can I touch. I feel a pang of guilt in my stomach but dismiss it.

"Are you sure I can do this, Grant? I've never been a secretary, I can barely work a copy machine at the FedEx store, and I don't know how to make coffee that doesn't come from a K-Cup."

"Mina, I know you can do this. You're young and trainable. If there's something you don't know, I can teach you. Oh, there are so many things I can teach you…" I trail off, growling softly. I catch myself, and it's my turn to be flustered. I clear my throat and continue. "What do you say, sweetheart? Ready to work for your dad's big, bad, best friend? I have a reputation for being a wolf in the bedroom..." I cough, catching myself once more. "I mean, in the boardroom. I am a wolf in the boardroom and expect nothing more than excellence from every member of the Wolf pack. Think you're up for the job?"

Mina smiles, her face lighting up the room like Christmas. "I'm up for it if you are, Uncle Grant."

Her calling me Uncle Grant once more sends shockwaves directly to my dick, and I have to force myself to stay seated and smile politely. I shouldn't look at Mina this way. I shouldn't think about her pretty pink lips wrapped around my cock. But when she says the word uncle, I have all sorts of impure thoughts.

"Perfect. When can you start?"

"I can start right away. I'm open tomorrow and..."

"No need to come in tomorrow. Monday morning is fine. I'll have your badge and onboarding papers made up, and they'll be ready when you walk in."

Mina suddenly stands up and bridges the small gap between us, throwing her arms around me. I find myself face first in her tits, smelling her soft, jasmine perfume and natural scent, and I get lost for a moment.

"Thank you, thank you so much, Uncle Grant!"

"No need to thank me, sweetheart. I'd do anything for you... Your dad, I mean. I'd do anything for your dad." I recover quickly as she pulls back. I stand up swiftly and reach out, grabbing her hand as she turns to collect her things.

"While you're here, why don't you and I grab a bite to eat? We can celebrate your new position, and I need a break from the office. We can hammer out the details of your internship. What do you say?"

She looks at me with uncertainty. "Are you sure you can get away? I don't want to keep you from anything important."

I grin at her, licking my lips. "Mina, I'm the fucking CEO. I can leave whenever I want."

Chapter Three

We take one of the company vehicles to lunch, and I hold the door for Mina. I watch as she slides onto the leather seats with graceful ease. Everything about her is graceful and tempting, and I have to put myself in my place with every moment we spend together. I shouldn't look at her like she's my next meal. I shouldn't have the kind of thoughts I've been having since she strolled into my office. For God's sake, she still calls me Uncle Grant. For all that she's grown, Mina is still very young, and I have to remind myself of that.

To distract myself on the long drive to the restaurant across town, I make small talk with Mina, trying to keep my eyes on the road and not on the length of her leg peeking out from her tight skirt. "So, Mina. We didn't finish catching up. I've hired you for your internship, but that can't be the only thing in your life. What do you do for fun? What's popular these days?"

Mina shifts in her seat, turning to face me. "Well, other than going to school, I don't do much for fun. I suppose there's my occasional yoga class at the rec center," she says, shrugging her delicate shoulders. From the corner of my eye, I see her breast illuminated by the sunlight streaming through the car window.

I refocus myself on the road and chuckle. "Yoga, huh? Do they still make you do the basics, like downward dog? My ex-wife was very fond of that one. In fact, I caught her doing downward dog with our lawyer. That's why she's my ex-wife."

Mina giggles. "So that's what happened to Aunt Carol."

I snicker. "That's what happened indeed. What about you, young lady? Is there a special man, or woman, in your life?" I pretend to be making friendly chit-chat, but what I really want to know is if anyone calls her their own. I want to know if there's a chance. I feel filthy even thinking these thoughts, but my mind is like a dog with a bone. It won't drop them no matter how hard I try to distract myself.

"No, there's no one."

"No? What do you mean? A girl as lovely as you should have a string of folks beating down your door to take you out on Friday night."

Mina shakes her head and sighs. "No one is interested in me, Uncle Grant."

"What the hell does that mean? Not interested in you?" I keep my eyes on the road, but my jaw begins to clench. I'm sure that's not the truth. I'm sure there are dozens of boys waiting to take her out and show her a good time.

"Well, I suppose it's because I'm still a virgin," Mina confides softly. At her admission, I almost crash the car but recover smoothly.

"I'm surprised the boys aren't more interested in you," I mumble and then catch myself. "Sorry, this is entirely inappropriate. We shouldn't be having this conversation. It's getting quite personal and, as your boss, it'd be an HR nightmare."

"It's okay. It's not like I'm saving myself for marriage or anything," she replies. She turns in her seat to face me once again. We're at a stoplight, and I turn my head to glance at her. Mina looks at me with a determined stare, her green eyes glowing in the afternoon sunlight.

"What? Why are you looking at me like that? Is there something on my face?" I chuckle and swipe a hand over my jaw.

"I was… I was hoping you could teach me, Uncle Grant," Mina says faintly, her words so gentle I almost don't hear them. When they wash over me and I catch her meaning, I cough, and it's my turn to turn red in the face.

"Teach you? Teach you what, exactly? I can teach you the business of Wolf Industries, I can teach you about finance and office management and—"

She cuts me off, reaching for my hand on the shifter. Her fingers tighten suggestively around mine. "I want you to teach me about sex."

"Didn't they cover that in private school? Surely you know about the birds and the bees. I'm sure you understand the general mechanics of the act." She has me thoroughly flustered, and I do my best not to steer us into oncoming traffic as she rubs her hand over mine.

"I know the basics, but that's all theory. I want you to… I

want you to show me in practice." Mina squares her shoulders and stares at me. I know she can see how hot under the collar I am. I loosen my tie at the next stoplight and glance at her, trying to read her face.

"Mina, darling. I've known your dad for longer than you've been alive. I wouldn't dream of…" I trail off, and she removes her hand from mine, tucking it into her lap. She turns her body away and stares out the window. In the reflection, I see her lower lip tremble. Teasingly, I mutter, "Sweetheart, don't pout. If you don't tuck that lower lip back in, I'll have to pull it right off."

"Maybe I'd like that," she retorts. She settles deeper into her seat but doesn't turn to face me again.

"You'd like that? Young lady, I am your father's best friend. Not to mention, I'm your boss now. Do you know the HR headache it'd cause if you got caught with your employer in a clinch?"

"You're not my boss until Monday."

"Are you getting sassy with me?"

"That depends. Do you like it when I get sassy, Uncle Grant?" She shifts and sits forward in the seat. Mina watches me thoughtfully as I weigh my next words carefully.

"No, I suppose until we sign the papers, I'm not your boss. Yet. I'm not your boss yet. But that still doesn't mean I'm going to… I'd never… Oh, fuck."

Mina reaches her hand across the console and runs her fingers up my thigh. She slides her fingers south and cups my cock through my slacks, giving me a firm squeeze. My foot freezes on the gas pedal, accelerating at a rapid rate. My eyes almost roll back in my head, and I let out a long, low growl.

"Remove your hand from my lap, Mina, before I crash this car."

She pulls away and looks hurt. She tucks her hand back into her lap, and, as she moves to turn away once more, I reach out and grab her shoulder, holding her in place. I ease up on the gas as we round the corner for the restaurant.

"Listen to me, Mina, I'm only going to say this once. I'm not going to pretend like seeing you in that pencil skirt and blouse doesn't have me nine shades of flustered. I've been imagining what color panties you have on and if they match the bra I can see through that incredibly sheer top. Oh, the things I've been dying to do to you all morning."

"What kinds of things?" Mina challenges me. Her voice is breathy like Marilyn Monroe, and her cheeks are flushed with desire. She shifts in her seat, her ankles crossing and uncrossing as she presses her thighs together.

"Filthy, deplorable, degrading things. Things that would end my friendship with your father."

"Maybe that's what I want, Uncle Grant." Oh, God, don't say that. Don't call me Uncle, not now.

My heart races, and my mouth goes dry thinking about the things I want to do to Mina. The positions I want to put her in, the clothes I want to dress her up in and peel her out of. I shouldn't, I know I shouldn't, but it's all I can think about. I want to make Mina mine, and only mine. I want to do things to her that will spoil her for other men, things that will keep her coming to my bed night after night. I want to give her the first time she deserves, the first time she craves. Mina is a virgin for a reason, and I think I know why.

We pull into the parking lot of the restaurant, and I choose a spot far, far away from the door.

"I shouldn't look at you this way. I shouldn't be talking to you like this. But when I see you sitting beside me, looking like the perfect mix of virgin and vixen, it's all I can do not to drive this car to the closest hotel. Corrupting you has been on my mind since the moment you stepped through my office doors, sweetheart. You came to me for a reason, didn't you? "

"Yes, Uncle Grant."

"Don't call me Uncle, baby girl. Uncles don't do to their nieces the things I'm going to do to you."

Mina sighs and shifts in her seat to face me, anticipation plain on her face. I know I'm going to give her what she wants.

"Is this how you imagined today would go, Mina? You'd come into my office and toy with me in that outfit? That I'd offer you a job, and you'd repay me by offering up your body? What did you think would happen, little girl?" I growl and her eyes widen, her breath catches, and her manicured nails dig into the leather seat.

She squares her shoulders and leans forward. Her shirt falls open at the top, exposing the tops of her breasts. Mina grabs my hand and pulls it to her chest, closing her fingers around mine. She squeezes my hand around her breast, and all pretense is dropped.

"Clearly, you don't know me as well as you thought, sweetheart. You're Little Red Riding Hood, and I'm the fucking wolf."

I lunge forward and pull her face to mine, capturing her lips in a searing kiss. It feels so wrong, but, in the same stroke, it feels so right. Her mouth mashes against mine as she grows bold, her tongue tracing the inside of my mouth. After several long, heated moments, Mina pulls away, looking at me with eyes as glazed as sea glass.

"Are you saying yes?"

I take a deep breath before I concede. "Yes. But first, we're going to have lunch. For all intents and purposes, I am your boss, and you are my employee. You're going to sit in my booth, be a proper young lady, and keep your hands to yourself. And when we're finished?"

Her eyes go wide, and she chews her lip as she looks at me hungrily. "When we're finished?"

"When we're finished, I'm going to take you home and fucking devour you, little girl. You want to learn about sex? You're about to get on-the-job experience. We're going to play nice at lunch and then I'm going to give you a lesson in taking dick…tation. Do you understand, Mina?"

She nods, her eyes wide as a sliver of her bubblegum-pink tongue traces her lips. "Good girl. Now, fix your face. I won't have my new assistant looking disheveled in my favorite restaurant. Not on her first day."

I shut off the car and step out, collecting myself with a deep, centering breath. I slyly adjust the front of my pants as I walk around to hold open the door for Mina.

They call me the big, bad wolf for a reason, and she's about to find out why.

Chapter Four

I struggle to keep my hands to myself during our luncheon. Everything Mina does is tinged with sexuality, from the way she sips her water to the way she eats her steak frites, cutting them into morsels and popping them into her mouth with the tiniest of moans. I keep myself together, but only barely, when she gets up from the table to go to the powder room, and I catch sight of her in that too-tight skirt. Her ass wiggles temptingly with every step. When she reaches the door, Mina turns and glances at me, her green eyes dark with anticipation. She winks as she pushes the wooden door open and steps inside, and I'm sure the entire restaurant can hear my exhalation.

It's exhausting, playing the charade of boss and employee, knowing what's waiting for me afterward. Knowing that for dessert, I'm skipping the crème brûlée and going straight for Mina's sweet, virgin pussy. The reasonable side of me tells me to make her first time special, to make it something she'll remember. The devil on my shoulder chimes in with a better idea: take her to the bathroom and give her something she'll really remember. The image plays through my head like a pornographic film, and I can almost hear Mina's sighs and moans from here. My pants grow uncomfortably tight, and I straighten in my seat.

Mina returns to our table, and I take a moment to collect myself from my explicit daydreams. I can't let on what I'm thinking of doing to her as soon as we're out of here. I clear my throat and drum my fingers on the table.

"Now, sweetheart, if we're going to do this, we're going to set some ground rules."

Mina's eyes grow wide, and she leans in conspiratorially. "What kind of rules?"

I lean forward, and a devious grin spreads across my face as I lay out the fine terms of our arrangement. "Rule number one. Your dad must never find out. Never, not even on his deathbed. Do you understand me?"

"Of course I understand. Do you think so little of me?" Mina crosses her arms over her chest, and her leg brushes mine under the table. Her foot glides up my ankle smoothly, and I shift away from her touch. She pouts, and I tut at her.

"No, I don't think little of you at all. I know you can keep a secret. But this is going to be the biggest secret of your life."

Mina nods and sips her wine, and I carry on to my next stipulation. "Rule number two. What happens between you and me is our business, and only our business. No one else in the company needs to know, least of all HR. I may be the CEO, but even I am not immune to an internal investigation."

I take a sip of my water and lay out the final detail, leaning forward and dropping my voice low enough so only Mina can hear me. "Third, and final, rule. You are never, ever allowed to call me Uncle Grant after today. 'Uncles' don't do what I'm going to do to you."

"And what are you going to do to me, Grant?" She challenges me with her eyes, and I accept it willingly. I keep my voice low between cool sips from my glass, my eyes never leaving hers.

"You weren't paying attention in the car, were you, Mina? As soon as I get you home, I'm going to eat you like the big, bad wolf I am. I'm going to peel you out of that skirt you've poured yourself into and teach you the finer points of pleasure. I'm going to eat the sweet little peach pussy that's dripping through your panties. I'm going to teach you how to ride my cock. And when we're done? I'm going to give you everything you've ever wanted."

"How do you know what I want?"

"Sweetheart, I've known you your entire life. You want one thing, and one thing only. Attention. And I intend to give you every shred of my attention and more."

Mina shivers and downs the last of the wine. "Get me out of here, Uncle Grant."

"Ah ah ah. What did I say, Mina? What were the terms of our agreement? You seem to need a refresher..."

She blushes and flusters, her gaze lowering like a naughty child. "Don't call you uncle?"

"Exactly. Try again."

"Get me out of here, Grant."

"Good girl. Let me settle our bill, and we'll be on our way." I wave the waitress over and slide her a crisp, one-hundred-dollar bill with a wink.

"Don't share that with the other girls," I tell her, and her eyes light up as she smiles at me.

"No, sir, Mr. Wolf."

"Please, call me Grant. Everyone does. Isn't that right, Mina?"

It's my turn to smile, and Mina looks even more like a naughty child caught in the act.

"Um, yes. That's precisely right, Grant." The way she stresses my name tells me Mina has only one thing on her mind. I watch her shift slightly in her seat and notice as she presses her thighs together. The subtle changes in her body language are slight and nearly imperceptible, but I take them in with a careful eye.

Mina is jealous of the waitress, and I can tell. It's almost cute, and I plan to use that to my advantage later. For now, all I need to do is get her home and out of that skirt.

I pay the tab and lead Mina to the car. We walk to the parking lot in near silence, the tension palpable between us. I know she's wondering what will happen next. I can't wait to show my pretty little pet everything I have in store for her.

I'm going to devour her.

I'm going to corrupt her.

I'm going to make her mine.

She just doesn't know it yet.

Chapter Five

I get Mina to the car and open the passenger door for her, the model of the perfect gentleman. I may be about to devour the poor girl, but I'll be damned if I'm not respectful. She slides into the seat gracefully, and I catch a flash of skin as her skirt rises up the length of her thigh. It's almost indecent, and I know she's doing this for my benefit. She was a perfect lady in the restaurant, the way her parents raised her, but now that we're alone? She knows she has my full attention and puts on a show for me.

As I walk around the front of the car, Mina unbuttons one button of her blouse. I watch as she traces the outline of her breast with one finger, trailing it around the curves with practiced ease. A low groan settles in my throat as I slip inside the car and take my seat next to her.

"Mina, if you keep playing with yourself in the car, I'll have to drive somewhere secluded and teach you a valuable lesson in discretion," I warn her sternly. I can't have us getting caught now. I can't have us getting caught ever.

"But Grant," she starts, and I interject, placing my hand on her knee.

"Trust me, Mina, it'll be worth the wait. We're not far from my house. Do you think you can be a good girl and keep your hands to yourself until then?"

She leans in and puts her lips to the shell of my ear. "It'll be awfully hard."

Her hand snakes between us and strokes the tip of my cock through my pants. I groan as I clasp my hand over hers and remove it, placing it back in her own lap.

"If you need to play with something, play with yourself," I say, trying to distract her.

"Is that a challenge, Grant?" Mina teases, and I look at her seriously.

"No, baby girl. That's an order." She gasps. Her cheeks burn pink when I call her baby girl, and I know I've found her sweet spot. I make a note to use that later, while I watch Mina squirm in her seat.

"I've never… I don't know how to…" She trips over her words, suddenly bashful and unsure of herself.

"You've never touched yourself?"

"No, I have. I've never… In front of anyone else."

"Oh? Not over FaceTime with a boyfriend?"

She mumbles her next words, but one thing sticks out to me. "I've never had a boyfriend."

"Do what I say, Mina. Just listen to my voice and follow my words."

She exhales the breath she's been holding. "Okay. Tell me what to do."

"Good girl. First, I want you to recline in your chair. Press the button on the side, and let it go all the way back."

From the corner of my eye, I watch her fiddle with the button and then her seat begins to recline.

"Next, I want you to unbutton your blouse. All the way."

She makes quick work of her blouse, letting it hang open and drape down her sides. I can see her nipples budding through the thin satin slip as the air conditioning blows across them.

"I want you to roll those pert tits between your fingers while you tell me what you like."

"What I like?"

"What you like. What do you think about when you're alone in bed? Do you have toys, Mina?"

Her breath shudders as she begins to roll her fingers around her hardened nipples.

"I have toys," she breathes.

"What kind of toys, baby girl? Tell me what you do when you're alone in the middle of the night."

Mina moans softly, and the sound runs straight to my dick. It twitches and begs to be set free, and I slide one hand from the wheel to palm myself.

"I have a dildo," she concedes.

"Yeah? I want you to slip one hand under your skirt. I want you to push those panties aside and slide one finger inside you."

Mina responds in kind, doing exactly as she's told. I look over and catch her in the act, pulling her skirt up her hips and pushing her hand beneath her stockings. She pushes her pink panties to the side and slips her finger inside her pussy.

"Tell me how you fuck yourself, Mina. Tell me everything."

I struggle to keep my eyes on the road as she slides her finger in and out of her wet pussy, a slippery sound filling the cab.

"I like to stick it on the edge of my bathtub and ride it," she pants.

"Do you play with your clit, baby?"

"Yeah," she whines, and I catch her circling herself with one practiced finger.

"So you like to fuck yourself on the bathtub and play with your clit… What else do you do, sweet little thing?" My voice is low and growly, and I watch as Mina arches her back.

"I like to fuck myself in the bathtub. I turn the faucet on and lay under it and…" Her voice trails off as she moans.

"Slip another finger inside yourself, baby." I press the accelerator as Mina follows my instructions. With my hand on my cock, I squeeze and thumb myself while I listen to her, trying to keep my eyes on the road when all I want is to watch my pretty little toy touch herself at my command.

I hear the wet sound as she slides her fingers in and out, picking up the pace as she rocks her hips into her hand. It fills me with animal need, and I take the turn onto my street a little too fast. Mina's moans fill my ears, and I groan, which only spurs her on. She fucks her fingers, hips bucking, sighing and moaning with pleasure. It's all I can do not to crash as I pull into the driveway. I park, shut off the car, and watch as Mina undulates against her hand.

"Stop."

"Uh?" She moans, and I reach out, placing my hand over

hers. She bucks and struggles against it, and I press down with a firm hand.

"Mina, stop. Stop fucking yourself. Save something for me."

Mina looks up at me, green eyes sparkling in the afternoon sun, and blinks slowly as though she doesn't understand.

"But I'm so close," she whines. I lean over the console and put my lips close to her ear. She pants with excitement as I lean in, and I can smell the arousal pouring off her skin in waves.

"I'm going to make you come, pretty girl. I'm going to be the only one who makes you come. Now, take your fingers out of your panties, fix your shirt, and let's go inside."

Chapter Six

Mina follows me inside after fixing her clothes and catching her breath. Her heels click on the floor, and she steps out of them as soon as she walks through my front door and into the foyer. She shrinks a solid two inches, and it makes me chuckle. I forgot who I was dealing with for a moment. Mina is my best friend's little girl, but she's also a grown woman with grown-woman needs. She's a grown woman, four inches shorter than me, and she's staring at me with lust in her eyes.

"Come here, baby girl. Give me a kiss," I command, wiggling my finger in a come-hither motion. Mina steps forward and puts her arms around my neck, rising on her tiptoes. I pull her close, pressing my body to hers so she can feel the hardness between us. I grind my hips into her, and she whimpers as my mouth comes down on hers.

She tastes sweet as sin and twice as damning. I shouldn't want this; I shouldn't want her. But the moment our lips touch and I taste the sweetness of her mouth, it's all I can think about. We kiss passionately, frantically, our hands exploring each other timidly at first but growing bolder by the moment. I snake my hands around her waist, under the hem of her shirt, and wrap my arms around her. Mina tangles her lithe fingers in my hair, tugging my head backward. She moves to kiss my throat, and I groan.

"Baby, I thought you said you were a virgin," I half-chastise, half-whimper. She nips at my Adam's apple and licks up my jawline to my ear lobe.

"I said I'm a virgin, but I didn't say I was inexperienced. I've learned a thing or two in college."

"Oh yeah, princess? And what did you learn?" I challenge her, my eyes rolling back in my head as she rakes her nails through my hair. Her hard nipples press against me through the thin layers of fabric between us, and I reach up to pinch them between my fingers. I roll them around and palm her breasts as she moans and whimpers, her legs growing unsteady beneath her. I wrap an arm around her and pull Mina closer.

She puts her cool hand on my cheek and caresses me, her fingers skittering over my stubble. She looks up at me with her big, green eyes, and I'm so captivated I almost miss her fingers working the clasp of my belt and undoing the button of my slacks.

"I know how to huff and puff and blow you."

"Baby girl, as much as I want to feel that sweet little mouth wrapped around my cock, I have other plans for you."

I grab her and spin her around, pressing her back into the wall. I grab her wrists in one of my large hands and pin them above her head, locking Mina in place. I stare down at her as she struggles and tries to fight her way out of my grasp, a smirk playing across my mouth.

"Settle down, Little Red. I told you, I'm the big, bad wolf for a reason. I'm going to eat you, I'm going to devour you, I'm going to leave you a quivering mess on this tile floor, and I'm going to make you beg me for more. The wolf always gets what he wants, and right now, princess? I want to watch you come undone."

I release my grip on her wrists, and Mina lowers her arms slowly, watching my every move carefully. My hands slide up her waist and over her ribcage, tugging on the tiny, pearl buttons of her blouse. They pop effortlessly, some of them falling to the floor and bouncing off the tile.

Mina gasps and shivers. "My shirt…"

"Baby, I'll buy you a hundred pearl-button shirts. With my money? I'll buy you whatever you need."

I rip her shirt out of the waistband of her skirt, and she wiggles out of it as I push it down her shoulders. I unzip her skirt at the back, fumbling with the tiny, metal slider like I'm in high school and she's my first lay. Eventually, the slider slides and Mina wiggles her hips, shimmying out of the tight fabric. She stands before me in a short, satin slip, seamed stockings, and a pair of pink panties.

I slide down her body to my knees, kneeling on the tile before her. Mina leans against the wall, jutting her hips out at me. The scent of her arousal smacks me in the face as Mina shudders and fidgets. I hook my fingers in the waistband of her stockings and tug, tearing the cream fabric away from her skin. I push the torn stockings down the length of her long, shapely legs and Mina steps out, kicking them aside.

"Touch me," she begs, her voice breathy with need.

"In due time, princess. You wanted a lesson in pleasure. That's why you came to me, after all, isn't it? You wanted me to teach you about sex, and I'm going to teach you everything I know. Your first lesson, baby girl, is to take it where you can get it."

I push the slip up past her hips and kiss her panty line. I push her panties aside and bury my face in her scent. Her soft pubic hair brushes against my stubble as I rub my face into her. Mina giggles, the sound ringing like a bell in my ears. I slide my mouth down to her slit and the giggles stop, replaced suddenly with harsh, shallow breaths. I look up at Mina one last time, winking at her before latching onto her pussy.

Mina's hand tangles in my hair as a make a meal out of her pussy, lifting one of her legs and putting it around my shoulder to grant me better access. I slide one thick finger inside her folds, and Mina cries out, her muscles clenching around my digit. I pump my hand slowly, letting her adjust to the feeling.

"Do you wanna fuck my finger, princess? Do you wanna ride it the way you ride your toys?"

Mina lets out a weak whimper, and I insert a second finger, stretching her pussy further around them. She's so slick with her desire that my fingers slip in and out with ease, curling and uncurling them inside her walls.

"Rock your hips, baby, ride my fingers."

"Uh-huh," Mina manages weakly, her hips beginning to rock against my hand. I slip my thumb between us and circle her clit, making Mina shudder and squeal. She picks up the pace while I slowly massage her swollen nub, pressing her pussy into my palm. The sounds of pleasure fill the air between us, the scent of desire thick in my nose. I lean forward and replace my thumb with my tongue, flicking it across her.

I could eat Mina's sweet pussy for breakfast, lunch, dinner, and a midnight snack. She tastes like peaches and cream, and she responds well to my touch. Her body undulates and bucks against me, and I know Mina is chasing her pleasure at warp speed. My baby girl wants to come undone, and I'll do everything to make it happen.

"Please?" Mina begs, her grip tightening in my hair.

"It's not up to me, precious. Your pleasure is up to you."

Her hips rock furiously against my hand, and I slide a third finger inside her sopping cunt. She whimpers as it stretches, her muscles contracting tighter around me.

Mina rocks into me one last time, nails scraping my scalp, and she lets out a long moan. She slows her movements and eases her grip, falling back against the wall. I slide my digits out from inside her sweetness and bring them to my lips for a taste. My eyes roll back in my head, and I groan as I taste her juices.

She begins to slide down the wall in a spent heap, and I reach up to catch her. She falls easily into my arms and puts her head on my shoulder, wrapping her arms around me.

"Did you like that, Little Red?"

She nods, unable to speak as she catches her breath. I stroke her back through the thin satin, and she turns her head to face me. Mina leaves a trail of kisses up my throat and jawline as she works her way to my ear lobe.

OLIVE SPENCER

She pauses her kisses to whisper in my ear. "Grant?"

"Yes, princess?"

"Take me upstairs."

Chapter Seven

I scoop Mina up in my arms and help her to her feet, guiding her up the stairs to my waiting bedroom. She's unsteady, and her legs shake as she takes the steps. I walk close behind to catch her if she slips. My hands never stray from her backside until we reach my room. Her slip hugs the curve of her ass, shifting and changing with each step.

Mina steps into my room and looks around, her eyes wide, mouth hanging open in an 'O' of surprise.

"It's so much bigger than I imagined."

"You have no idea, princess." I chuckle as I slide under the slip and run my fingers around the waistband of her panties, sliding them down and cupping her pert ass. I drag my fingers down the cleft of her cheeks and tap my finger around her entrance. Mina sucks in a deep breath, her body going rigid. I lean into her and brush my lips against the shell of her ear.

"Relax, baby girl. I'm just exploring. Take these off and let me see all of you."

Mina does as she's told. She pulls the thin satin slip over her head, freeing her gorgeous, round tits. She slips out of the pink panties and lets them pool on the floor. I bend over and pick them up, tucking them in my pocket. I want a trophy of this afternoon, to remember it for the rest of my life.

Mina's body is a work of art. Curves in the right places, her skin as soft as cashmere, her green eyes glowing with desire. I watch as her breasts heave with every labored, anxious breath. Her belly, so soft, trembles when I slide my palm over her skin.

I guide Mina over to the bed and help her sit. I kick off my shoes and push them under the bed. Mina looks up at me with big, expectant eyes as I tuck my hand under her chin. I lower my face to hers and capture her lips in a searing kiss. She moans into my mouth as I guide her backward onto the mattress until my body dwarfs hers. I perch over her, staring into her eyes, watching her shift and squirm.

"Baby, what happens next is up to you."

"What do you mean?"

"I don't want to fuck you because you think that's what I want. I want to fuck you because it's what you want. Do you understand me?"

She swallows and nods, her green eyes never leaving mine.

"Mina, if you want this to happen, I need to hear you say it. I need you to tell me what you want, baby girl."

Her hand slides up my side and knots in the fabric of my shirt. Mina brings her legs up on either side of my hips and squeezes me closer.

"I want it. I want you."

"What do you want me to do?"

"I want you to fuck me, Grant."

I groan as she utters the magic words, a shiver rolling down my spine in waves. Who am I to tell her no?

"Your wish is my command, princess."

I slide my hands under her back and scoop Mina into my arms, crawling backward as I lift her. I sit her up and put her hands on my belt.

"Undress me, baby. I want to see the look in your eyes when you see my cock for the first time," I growl. Mina shivers and begins pulling my belt through the loops. She drops it to the floor and tugs my zipper, pushing my pants down my ass. I'm hard as a steel beam, ready to burst out of my boxers. Mina looks up at me with big, expectant eyes as she hooks her fingers into the waistband and tugs. The gasp that escapes her lips sends a wave of pleasure through me.

"My, what a big cock you have," she whispers, staring at it as though she's never seen a dick before.

I grin down at her and run my fingers through her hair. "I do all right for myself."

Mina trails one finger along my shaft and swirls it around the tip, dripping pre-cum and throbbing at her light touch. I make quick work of the buttons of my shirt, shrugging it off my shoulders and letting it fall to the floor. Mina pulls her eyes away from my member for a moment as I tug my undershirt over my head, and she runs her fingers through the trail of hair that leads up my belly.

"Do you like what you see, princess?"

She nods, chewing her lip.

"Am I everything you imagined I'd be, Mina?"

"Everything and more, Uncle Grant."

Her words wash over me, and her face burns bright red as she realizes what she's said. "I'm sorry, I didn't mean to!"

"It's okay, baby girl. Just this once, I'll let it slide," I reassure her. I dip to press a kiss to her forehead, and Mina leans into my kiss. "It's okay to be nervous, sweetheart."

"I'm not nervous!" Her voice rises, betraying her words.

"Yes, you are. It's okay, Mina, I'll be gentle with you.

"You promise?"

"I do. Now, where were we?"

I grab her hand and put it back on my shaft, and Mina strokes me reverently. She runs her fingers along my length and toys with the head before lowering her mouth to take me inside. The sensation courses through me like a tsunami, hitting me in waves of pleasure, astonishment, and pleasure again. Mina sucks my cock, her head bobbing slowly along it, her tongue gliding along my member as though she's done this hundreds of times. My eyes roll back in my head when she takes me deeper inside her mouth, her hand fisting against my leg.

I know that trick. The anti-gag-reflex, thumb-in-a-ball trick. I open my eyes and look down, seeing the look of concentration on Mina's face. Slowly, I pull back and ease out of her mouth, hearing her small groan of disappointment as I withdraw.

"Baby, baby, baby," I coo, stroking her cheek with my thumb. "You don't have to swallow me whole. We'll build up to that, but for now? Baby steps."

Mina nods and moves forward to take me back in her mouth. As much as it pains me, I pull away. I shake my head and click my tongue at her. "Sweetheart, what did I just say?"

"Don't swallow you whole?"

"Exactly, princess. There will be time for you to suck my cock later. But right now? There's only one thing on my mind, and that's being buried in your pussy."

Mina bites her lip and tucks a strand of hair behind her ear. "Still nervous?"

She hesitates before speaking, looking up at me with her big green eyes. "I'm not on birth control. You can't come in me."

I take a step toward my nightstand and open the drawer, rustling around for a condom. I find one and pull it out, grinning at her.

"Feel better now?" I step forward, tugging open the silver foil packet. "I want you to put this on me. I trust you, do you trust me?"

Mina nods and reaches for the condom, her hands shaking slightly. My fingers find hers, steadying the tremble.

"Just breathe, princess. Grab my cock, roll it down the tip. All the way to the base. Good girl. Good girl." Mina follows my instructions, and her cheeks burn carnation pink as my words roll over her. When I'm fully sheathed, she looks up at me expectantly, licking her lips.

"Now what?"

"Now, you lie back and let me take care of you."

Chapter Eight

I crawl up Mina's body as she finds her position in bed, her legs parting like the gates of Heaven before me. I stroke my cock as her waiting wetness is revealed, the scent of desire thick in the air.

"Look how wet you are, princess. Do you always get this wet when you play with yourself? Do you get this hot when your dildo is sliding into that pretty pussy of yours?"

Mina looks up at me, eyes dark, and shakes her head. "Only when I think of you."

"And how long have you been thinking of me in bed?"

"All my life."

I shudder and groan, the low rumble stirring something inside me. "All your life, baby? Is that why you've never had a boyfriend?"

"I wanted you to be my first, Grant," she admits, stroking my arm.

I spit on my fingers and slide my hand across her slit, warming her up for my cock. She's so slick, so ready, and, if I wait another moment, I won't be able to control myself.

"Tell me what you want, Mina."

"I want you, Grant. I want you inside me."

"Your wish is my command, precious."

I line the head of my cock up with her entrance and push inside slowly, allowing her time to adjust. Her pussy is so warm around me, and I can't stop the flood of obscenities that pour from my lips. Mina shifts beneath me as my cock slides deeper inside her, filling her in ways she's never been filled before.

"Does that feel good, baby?"

She nods, eyes screwed shut.

"Does it hurt?"

"No."

"Do you want me to go faster?"

"Uh-huh. Please fuck me," she whimpers, her hips beginning to rock forward on my cock.

"Easy, sweetheart. Let me take care of you."

I set the pace, thrusting into her slowly, pulling out and pushing in like the waves of the ocean coming ashore. It's painfully slow for me. I want to pound into her pussy, I want to fuck her hard and fast. I want to have her scream my name over and over again, but I remind myself—all in due time.

Mina's hands snake up my arms, fingers tracing the soft definition of my muscles before wrapping them around my head and pulling me closer.

"Faster, please," she whispers in my ear, voice heavy with need. I pick up speed, slamming into her, the sound of her moans and skin on skin filling the air. She digs her nails into my shoulder as she bucks her hips into me, fucking me back.

"Whose pussy is this, Mina?"

She looks up at me, her wide eyes gone hazy. "Yours."

"That's right," I mutter approvingly. "And whose body is this?"

"Yours," she replies, crying out in pleasure as I thrust into her over and over.

"I'm going to fuck you into the mattress, pretty girl. I'm going to fuck you so deep you ache for my cock for days. You're going to cry out for me in the night. You're going to toss and turn, and your toys won't fill the void I'm going to leave," I pant, chest heaving with each word.

"Please, Uncle Grant!" she cries out, and it ignites something primal inside me. I fuck into her harder, grabbing her wrists and pinning them over her head. I pound into her sweet, wet cunt faster, my climax building with each stroke.

"Say it again, princess."

"Please!"

"No, baby. Say it again."

She licks her lips and looks me dead in the eye. "Uncle Grant."

"Yes, baby, yes."

I slide my dick out and tell her to roll onto her side. Mina whines as I withdraw but does as she's told, turning over. I position myself behind her, grabbing her round, bubble ass and gripping her firmly.

"Tell me how badly you want my dick, sweetheart. Tell me how you need me to make you my own."

"I need it so bad. Please, please, please," she whimpers. I catch her rubbing her clit, and I reach over and cover her hand with my palm. Her fingers stop moving beneath me, and I take her hand in mine, rubbing circles around the engorged nub.

"Anything for you, my pretty little plaything. Show Uncle Grant how you play with your pussy while I fuck you," I growl in her ear. Fuck it, if we're going to do this, I'm going to give in. Call me uncle, baby.

I slide my cock inside her, and she moans, her muscles contracting around me in a vice-like grip. "You take my cock so well, princess. You feel so good wrapped around me," I reassure her.

"Uncle Grant," she whimpers, her hand in mine picking up pace as we stroke her clit together. I rock my hips into her slowly, letting her pleasure build to its peak.

"Are you gonna come for me, baby girl?"

She manages a weak response before her muscles contract tighter around me. I pick up my pace inside her while Mina continues rubbing her clit furiously.

"Come for me, princess. Show your uncle how you come with his dick inside you."

Mina's core contracts around my cock, milking it for all its worth. Her moans of pleasure ring in my ear as I pump inside her, skin slapping against skin.

"Come for me, Mina, come for me," I groan. I'm chasing my own orgasm while I thrust inside her sweet little cunt, each stroke pushing me closer and closer to the edge of release.

"Oh, God!"

Mina chases her pleasure and her fingers still while her muscles contract around my cock. I push inside her twice before my own climax comes crashing down on me, hitting me like a ton of bricks. I shut my eyes and call out her name as pinpricks of pleasure invade my senses. I've never come this hard. It rocks my world, tilting me off my axis as I recover. The world stops spinning and all that matters is Mina in my arms.

Chapter Nine

After a few moments of silence, punctuated only by the sound of heavy breathing, I finally find my voice.

"How was that, sweetheart? Did it live up to your expectations?"

"I never knew sex would be like that."

"Like what?"

"Earth-shattering."

I groan as I withdraw from inside her, rolling onto my back. Mina whimpers, and I pull her to me, tucking her under my arm and close to my chest.

"It's not always earth-shattering, princess, but that? That was something else." I stroke her back as we lay tucked into each other and listen to her breathe. It's the most peaceful I've felt in years.

"Grant?"

"Yes, baby girl?"

"What… What happens now?"

I look down at her, Mina's big, green eyes gazing up at me

with uncertainty. I can tell she's nervous. I can tell she's uneasy about what this means for her internship and our relationship.

"Nothing changes, baby. Or, at least, it doesn't have to change. Your position at Wolf is secure. You'll be my new secretary if you still want to."

"I want to."

"Good." I kiss her forehead. "Nothing has to change, Mina, just because we've seen each other naked. We can go on as boss and employee, or we can go on as long-time family friends. No one will ever know what happened here. It'll be our little secret."

"What if..."

"What if what?"

"What if we do this again?"

"Do you want to do this again, sweetheart? Do you want to find yourself in my bed again?"

Mina is silent for a moment. She runs her hand up my chest, tangling her fingers in the soft hair between my pecs.

"I do. I want to do this over and over and over. But I'm afraid you'll never look at me the same. I'm afraid you'll never see me the same ever again." Her voice is soft, and her concern is sincere. She's right. From today, I'll no longer see the little girl my best friend raised. I'll never see the shy teenager, peeking her head into her dad's office while we have cigars and scotch. I'll never see the girl on graduation day, her smile as big and as bright as the sun. From now on, I'll only see a woman. I'll only see her as mine.

"You're right. I'm never going to look at you the same. Whenever I see you, I'm going to think of the way you look with my dick buried in you. I'm going to smell the sex rolling off your every pore. The heat, the musk, the soft scent of roses. It's burned into my brain."

I scoop her into my arm and roll her onto my chest, her body flush against mine.

"I'm going to have the taste of that sweet, juicy pussy on my tongue long after you're gone. I'll be in the boardroom, licking my lips at the memory of your quim dribbling down my chin. Sweetheart, you're going to be more than just my secretary. You're going to be my star employee."

Mina kisses me quickly, roughly, full of heat, and I ease her away gently.

"Baby girl, we don't have time for round two."

"Why?"

I struggle to find an acceptable answer. "We should probably get dressed and get you back to the office. You have papers to sign, and I have arrangements to make. I'm not going to let you out of my sight, sweetheart."

"No?"

"No. I want to keep you nearby at all times. A good secretary learns to anticipate her employer's needs. I'm going to teach you how to be the best."

"What happens after that?"

"I'm going to devour you, sweetheart. I'm going to make you mine in every way that matters."

Mina shivers, her petite form vibrating against me. "What about my dad?"

"Your dad never needs to find out I deflowered his little girl. When he asks how your internship is going, I'll give him nothing but a glowing review of your... performance."

Mina blushes, and I reach up my hand to stroke her cheek. She eases into my touch and closes her eyes.

"Baby girl, go get dressed. I'm going to take you back to the office, then you're going to go home. I'm going to finish out my workday, and tomorrow? The real fun begins."

I roll Mina onto her back and lean over her, dwarfing her frame.

"Grant?"

"Yes, princess?"

"I can't wait to work for you." She kisses my cheek and looks so innocent, I almost forget the dirty things I've done to her.

"Me either, baby girl. Now, go find what's left of your clothes. I'll drop you off at your car, so no one sees you in disrepair. I'd hate to ruin your reputation before you've even started."

I give her one last kiss before sliding out of bed and making my way to the restroom. As I reach the door, I turn and look, seeing my best friend's daughter spread naked in my bed. I've never seen anything more beautiful; I've never seen anything more captivating. I'm going to have her in my bed again. I'm going to have her in my bed tomorrow night and the night after.

I'm going to devour my Little Red and make her mine in every way. My employee, my plaything, my princess. She just doesn't know it yet.

Epilogue

Mina settles into her position as my secretary while Gladys is away. She brings me the perfect cups of coffee, arranges my schedule, and keeps the offices of Wolf Industries in tip-top shape. She handles the phone with grace, takes precise dictation, and is an asset to the company I've built from the ground up. Despite her reservations, Mina learned to use a copier and the espresso machine. She took to her role quickly, and I couldn't be more proud.

On Fridays after work, when everyone has gone home, Mina stays behind to go over the week's work. Or that's the story we give the rest of the staff. No one knows precisely what goes on behind the closed mahogany door. There are rumors of impropriety, and there are whispers of Mina being groomed to take over Gladys' position full time. We never let on what really happens once the door shuts and the staff clears out.

I fuck Mina on my desk, pounding into her pussy with clandestine fervor. I fuck Mina in my leather chair, letting her ride my cock until she comes, her juices trickling down my legs. I eat Mina's pussy while she sits behind my desk, her high heels perched on the glass blotter, her fingers tangled in my hair. I give Mina pleasure like she's never felt before, making up for all the years she wanted me and I was powerless to please her.

I make sure she leaves the office in exactly the same condition she came in, straightening her clothes with care and fixing the smeared lipstick and black mascara streaks after she sucks my cock. She looks so beautiful with my dick in her mouth, it takes all I have not to burst the moment she wraps her lips around me. Her oral skills are unmatched, and I wonder what else she learned in college.

Late one Friday after work, after all the other employees have left, Mina is curled up in my arms, laying on the boardroom table. The scent of sex is heavy in the air, as is the scent of the rose perfume she wears specifically for me. My pretty plaything knows exactly what I like, and I reward her in kind for her attention to detail.

Mina sits up and slides off the table, her perky, round ass jiggling with each step. She wraps herself in my suit coat and stares out the window of the high-rise, looking out over the city. The sun begins to set, lighting her in oranges and purples, and I've never seen anything more beautiful.

"What am I going to do when you go back to school in September, baby girl?" I ask, sliding beside her and nuzzling my face into her hair.

"We'll cross that bridge when we get to it. What am I going to do this weekend while you're gone?"

I consider her a moment, watching the sunset paint her face

in lovely shadow as the sun sinks behind the other high-rises.

"You could come with me. I'll make up an excuse to tell your father, something about it being a work trip?"

Mina laughs softly, the sound slightly musical as she rests her head on my shoulder. "D'you really think Daddy would go for that?"

"Of course he will. Your father knows how important the, ah, work you do around here is. Besides, don't you know by now, princess? I always get what I want." I slide my hand beneath the hem of my suit coat and cup Mina's ass. I slowly knead the firm flesh, and, in moments, I have Mina purring in my ear.

"Are you sure I won't be a hindrance to your weekend?"

I shake my head as my hand slides down the cleft of her ass. I find the entrance to her pussy, still wet, and push one finger inside her. Mina shudders, drawing in a harsh breath through her teeth. I rock my hand and slip another finger inside her.

"Mina, come with me. This weekend, come with me. Don't make me huff and puff and blow your house down, Little Red."

She whimpers at her nickname, or perhaps it's the fact that I've picked up the pace of my fingers in her cunt. I slide my free hand around her belly, down her mound, and thumb her clit, playing her like a fiddle. I feel her second orgasm of the night begin to build, and I put my lips to her ear, whispering.

"Come with me. Come for me. Spend the night in my bed, princess. I want to wake up next to you, just once. I want to wake up and slowly fuck the sleep out of you. What do you say, baby girl? Are you going to come?"

She pants and whimpers as her core contracts. She's close. I kiss her neck and increase the pressure on her clit.

"Don't think, baby, just say yes."

I slide my fingers out one last time and then push them inside her pussy, hard and fast, making Mina rock back and forth.

"Yes!" she cries out as her orgasm washes over her. Her body tenses, and her pussy clenches around my fingers, milking them the way it milks my cock when I'm buried to the hilt inside her. Her legs wobble, and I steady her, my arm around her waist. I withdraw my fingers, sticky with her love, and put them to her lips. Mina laps up her juices like a kitten, and I'm sure the groan that escapes my lips can be heard throughout the city.

"You'll come with me, then. Go home and pack a bag. I'll call your father. I'll arrange everything," I assure her. I slide my jacket down her shoulders and throw it on the table. I stoop and reach for her clothes, laying them on the table as she gets dressed. I follow suit, dressing in a hurry, digging for my phone in one of my pockets.

Mina dresses and straightens her hair and makeup in a compact mirror. She's so messy, so beautiful. I take her mouth in one last, searing kiss before she leaves.

"Oh, and baby?"

"Yes, Uncle Grant?" She says it sweetly, and it sends a bolt of lightning straight to my cock.

"Pack something silky you don't mind losing. If I'm going to tear you out of your clothes the moment we reach the hotel room, I don't want to feel guilty for ruining them."

"Yes, Uncle Grant."

Mina strides out of the room in her heels and tight skirt, and I feel a piece of my heart walk out with her.

I didn't want to fall in love with my best friend's daughter, and yet, here I am.

OLIVE SPENCER

Acknowledgements

Once again, I want to thank my friends in a very specific Discord server for encouraging me to write.

I am eternally grateful to the makers of Diet Coke, for without their nectar of the gods, I would not have had been able to focus long enough to get Grant and Mina's story on the page.

I owe a large debt to the creators of Youtube, my friends on Twitter, and the few people in real life who know who Olive Spencer is.

For everyone on Radish, this one is for you.

Thank you, each and every one of you.

About the Author

The Wolf series is one of Olive's favorite tales to date. The idea for the story came from an unused script in her former life as an erotic audio scriptwriter. Having retained the rights to the story, Olive felt it was finally time to release The Wolf and see where the story takes her.

Olive Spencer writes contemporary, and sometimes paranormal, erotic fiction. When Olive is not busy behind the screen of her trusty MacBook, you can find her with a Diet Coke in hand while watching a soap opera, or wandering around a local bookstore with her headphones on.

She's probably listening to a spicy audiobook, or her favorite country song, 'Dicked Down in Dallas'.

Olive is not a Gemini vegetarian, but she is a fan of all things Reese Witherspoon.

Where to find Olive Online

Olive Spencer loves Twitter! Please consider joining her at @misskmagpie and sending her a tweet.

She also thrives on the sense of community and encouragment that comes from publishing on Medium.
Join her at www.olivespencer.medium.com and see what all the fuss is about. If you liked Ghosted and Blood Lust, make sure you read her sleep demon stories!

If you want to visit her website, you can find Olive online at www.olivespencer.com.

Thank You

If you're read this far, you deserve a cookie, a glass of warm milk, and a blanket. Thank you so much.

This is just the beginning of Grant and Mina's story. I hope you stick around for part two.

www.ingramcontent.com/pod-product-compliance
Lightning Source LLC
LaVergne TN
LVHW061048070526
838201LV00074B/5225